Mischa Damjan

THE MAGIC PAINTBRUSH

Illustrated by Janosch

North-South Books

Many years ago, when animals knew how to talk to children, a small boy named Philip used to visit the old pony who lived next door. The pony belonged to Rosalia, who had a fruit and vegetable stall in the market, but because the pony was too old and sick to carry heavy loads, she no longer took care of him.

One day Philip came to visit his friend, while Rosalia was at the market. He brought some oats and some juicy beets, and the pony was delighted. "It is time to give you something in return," said the pony. "What would you like?"

Philip thought for a while, and then he said, "What I would really like is a magic paintbrush."

The old pony laughed, showing all his yellow teeth, and told Philip to cut a tuft of hair from his mane to make the paintbrush. "Now you will be able to paint anything you want. If you paint a blade of grass, everyone will think it is really a blade of grass, and if you paint a fire, everyone will think it is a real fire."

That evening Philip could not go to sleep for a long time. He put the paintbrush under his pillow and thought of all the things he could do with it. He might paint the old pony to look like a zebra and then give him to the zoo, where he would be well looked after. Philip soon gave up that idea, though. But he might change a sparrow into a canary or a raven into a bird of paradise! Then he remembered his pony friend's words: "If you paint a fire, everyone will think it is a real fire." Now Philip knew what he would do to punish Rosalia in the morning. He fell happily asleep.

Next morning Rosalia set out for the market, to look after her fruit and vegetable stall, as she always did. She had to carry her own basket as the pony was sick. Philip watched her go, and when she was out of sight, he crept out of his house.

He took some fire-red paint and painted one of the windows in Rosalia's house. When he had finished, he stepped back and looked at his handiwork carefully. It looked just like a real fire, and flames seemed to be licking up behind the window. "It certainly is a magic paintbrush!" thought Philip with satisfaction, and he ran home.

In the afternoon Rosalia came back from the market as usual. When she reached her yard and saw the flames at the window, she stopped in terror. "Help, help, my house is on fire!" she shouted, and she ran screaming all the way to the market to get help.

It was not long before ten brave firemen were rushing toward the house in a big red fire engine. The moustaches of the firemen waved in the breeze, and the great bell tolled, "Alarm, alarm!" In no time the fire engine was ready, the hose was unrolled, and the men began to pump.

The chief fireman spun his enormous moustache in the wrong direction and murmured to himself, "A fire without smoke? No, that never happens!" Then, as the fire-red paint ran down the window, everyone realized what was the matter. The firemen got ready to leave, but they were so muddled and embarrassed by their mistake that they drove off backwards in their big red fire engine.

That evening, Philip thought up a new trick to play on Rosalia, and he fell happily asleep thinking about it.

In the morning, as soon as Rosalia left for market, Philip slipped into her henhouse and painted black spots on all the white hens. Then he chased them all out into the yard and ran home.

When it was time for Rosalia to come home, Philip climbed into the walnut tree. From there he could see the whole of Rosalia's yard but she couldn't see him.

As soon as Rosalia noticed the spotted hens, her eyes opened wide. "Strange hens in my yard?" she cried furiously. "Get out — shoo!" And she chased them out. Then she went to look in the henhouse, but it was empty. Rosalia looked around for her own hens, but all she could see were the spotted ones which had come back into the yard and were scratching for worms. "*Could* those be my hens after all?" she asked herself, and she began to be frightened. "Everything seems to be bewitched," she said, shaking her head as she went into the house.

As Philip lay in bed that evening, trying to think of another trick, he remembered that some time ago Rosalia had lost her canary. The bird, who was a wonderful singer, had flown away, and although Rosalia had looked for him every day, had asked all her friends, and had even advertised in the newspaper, he had never been found. Now Philip knew what he would do next, even though this trick would be more difficult than the earlier ones.

In the morning, as soon as it was light, he went off to the birdseller, who lived behind the market-place, and had all kinds of birds to sell — everything from a wren to a sparrow. Philip bought a common street sparrow and ran home.

He took some bright yellow paint, and in no time he had turned the sparrow into a beautiful canary. At midday, while Rosalia was at the market as usual, Philip slipped through her kitchen window, where the birdcage was still hanging. He gently opened the door of the cage and put the sparrow inside.

Rosalia was beside herself with joy when she noticed the bird that afternoon. She told all her friends and acquaintances, "My bird has come back, my bird has come back. He came back after seven whole days and nights, and he even opened the cage door himself."

Her joy was so great that soon half the village appeared in her yard, to see the remarkable bird who could open his own cage and to hear him sing.

They all stood and waited for the bird to sing with pleasure at being home again. But he didn't seem to want to sing. Everyone waited patiently, and after a long time the bird stretched his neck and cheeped a couple of times. But of course he sounded just like a street sparrow. Rosalia turned pale. What was wrong? No one knew what to say, and they kept perfectly quiet, waiting to see what would happen next. Philip, who had hidden himself at the back of the crowd, decided it was time for him to leave. Then the sparrow shook himself and said, "Cheep, cheep, chee-cheep, cheep!" He was excited by the crowd of people.

Everyone began to laugh. They laughed as though they would never stop until Rosalia took down the cage. "Everything seems to be bewitched," she murmured as she slammed the door behind her visitors.

But Philip's tricks were at an end. The next day Rosalia discovered him in the henhouse, starting to paint the eggs. Philip had to confess to his parents and Rosalia what he had been doing. When they asked why he had done so much mischief, he explained that he had played these tricks on Rosalia because of the way she had neglected the poor old pony. Rosalia was ashamed because she knew that he was right and that she had treated the pony badly.

So Rosalia and Philip made peace. Philip wanted to put his mischief right, so he polished all the windows of Rosalia's house until they sparkled in the sun. He curried the pony twice a week, too, but this was not a harsh punishment. Every day Philip could see the old pony, with just a couple of baskets on his back, trotting happily to market.

First published in Great Britain, Canada, Australia
and New Zealand in 1968 by Dobson Books Ltd and reissued
in 1988 by North-South Books, an imprint of Rada Matija AG.

Distributed in Great Britain by
Blackie and Son Ltd, 7 Leicester Place,
London WC2H 7BP.
British Library Cataloguing in Publication Data

Damjan, Mischa
The magic paintbrush.
I. Title   II. Janosch   III. Filipo und
sein Wunderpinsel. *English*
833'.914[J]   PZ7

ISBN 0-200-72937-3
ISBN 0-200-72938-1 Pbk

Distributed in Canada by
Editions Etudes Vivantes, Saint-Laurent.

Distributed in Australia and New Zealand by
Buttercup Books Pty. Ltd., Melbourne.
ISBN 0 949447 76 5 (hardcover)
ISBN 0 949447 77 3 (paperback)

Printed in Germany